The Good
RAINBOW ROAD

RAWA 'KASHTYAA'TSI HIYAANI

The Good
RAINBOW ROAD

RAWA 'KASHTYAA'TSI HIYAANI

A Native American Tale in Keres and English

Followed by a Translation into Spanish

Simon J. Ortiz

ILLUSTRATIONS BY Michael Lacapa

Spanish translation by Victor Montejo

This book is published in collaboration with Oyate.

THE UNIVERSITY OF ARIZONA PRESS

Tucson

For Sara, my daughter, so she and all other children of the earth
may always walk the good rainbow road.

And for my grandchildren Krista, Desirray, Monique, Tayo, and Chayson.

The University of Arizona Press
© 2004 Simon J. Ortiz
First printing
All rights reserved
∞ This book is printed on acid-free, archival-quality paper.
Printed in China
09 08 07 06 05 04   6 5 4 3 2 1

Library of Congress Cataloging-in-Publication Data
Ortiz, Simon J., 1941–
   The good rainbow road / Simon J. Ortiz ; illustrations by Michael Lacapa ;
Spanish translation by Victor Montejo.
      p.   cm.
"Published in collaboration with Oyate."
In English, Keres, and Spanish.
Summary: An account of two boys who are sent by their people to the west to visit the Shiwana, the spirits of rain and snow,
and bring back rain to relieve a drought.
   ISBN 0-8165-2340-1 (alk. paper)
   1. Acoma Indians—Juvenile fiction. [1. Acoma Indians—Fiction.   2. Rainbow—Fiction.   3. Indians of North America—
New Mexico—Fiction.   4. Polyglot materials.]   I. Lacapa, Michael, ill.   II. Montejo, Victor, 1951–   III. Title.
[Fic]—dc22
                                                                           2003014279

British Library Cataloguing-in-Publication Data
A catalogue record for this book is available from the British Library.
Publication of this book is made possible in part by the proceeds of a permanent endowment created with the assistance of a
Challenge Grant from the National Endowment for the Humanities, a federal agency.

A T THIS TIME which is four hundred years after the beginning of the European colonization of our Indigenous people, this story is especially for our people who remain as always one with our land, culture, and community. Yes, always the land, culture, and community; always the people sustained with love, compassion, prayer, hope, courage, humility; always a belief in our sacred sovereignty; always the healing belief in ourselves.

We must always look back at the good way our people have lived and the good road they have traveled. We must always look upon the sacred knowledge that has helped our people. Not only must we remember, but we must live the healthy, good way of tradition and culture. In this way, we will always continue as a strong and healthy people.

Sʀᴜ ʜᴀɪ'ᴋᴜᴍɪɪ ᴋᴀᴛʏᴀᴍᴀ nu"te"kani"kuyase
sutrusa "kuuwa 'yuwesra hanu 'koname "te'emi
"kuu rawa hiyaani "te"kuyani. Sru hai'kumii
hotyinu"te"k'ani"kuyase sutrusa 'kaasrka 'kayatyuni.
"Tueu hanu tsaiwaamaatsani. Tsatsi nuue
niiuwaatyumishe sr"kusa, esr"ku n'un'atsa sr"kune
ewanu"te"kuya'a"ta sutrusa, "kuu ewa hanu
"tiuwahimashe ewa nu"te"kuya'a"ta sutrusa.
Srue "taawa nishaatsi sutrusa "kuu n'un'atsa
sutrusa.

Many, many years ago,
there was a village at the foot of Haapaahni Quuti.
The mountain was called that, Haapaahni,
because of the oak trees that grew there.
And the village, therefore, was named for it,
Haapaahnitse, Oak Place.
Near Haapaahnitse, there used to be a lake,
and flowing into it there used to be a stream.
But now there was no longer a lake,
and there was no more flowing stream;
they had dried up many years before.
And now they were dry because for many years
it had not rained and it had not snowed.

Yuwee hama
aiinutsiyaa 'Kuuti H'apani ha'as'titrata.
'Kuuti H'apani e'ta'aneukuyasi,
tsaami aii h'apani chiwa euheya 'kuuti h'apani
        e'ta'aisratrane.
"Kuu srue ha'a'stiitra e'ta'aisratrane.
H'apani.
Aii'e H'apanitse sranu tyuwai,
"kuu hawe sranu chiina 'tisrpiiya'ata.
Esrku tsatsina ainu tyuwai
"kuu tsatsina 'tisrpiiya'a'ta;
srumiisru maanu kasraiti ainu "kuwaisruma 'tipanitu.
Sru ts'ii'kami kasraiti t'epani,
tsatsina chacha "kuu tsatsina chawetu.

The people of Haapaahnitse
had raised corn, squash, beans, and chili
on lands near the lake,
and they had watered their plants
from the stream when it had flowed.
Because they had not lacked for anything
and had plenty to eat, they had been
    happy.
But for a long, long time the rain and
    snow
had not come, and the land had grown
    dry.
When the people planted seeds of corn,
the plants grew only so tall, then they
    dried.
Squash sprouted and their vines spread,
but they shriveled under the hot, hot sun,
and soon they died; every plant was dying.
Even the strong and hardy oak trees,
which the village was named for, were
    dying.

H'apanii'mee
'yaa'ka, "kuu "taani, "kuu "kanami, "kuu chiiri
    chawati
ainu ha'a'tsi "kuwaisr'umishru
'kawaiti chu'washchuw'ane
na 'tsisrpii'ya'a"to.
Tsatsiti "tewi
"kuu 'nau 'u"pewi "ta, "tiu'wawistiya.
Esrku tsi'ii"kami tsatsi kachani "kuu hawe
tsatsi tya'a'tsi, sai ha'a'tsii "tipanitu.
Sru tsina hanu "yaa"ka chaawaa"timetyo,
tsatsi hawi"trana tya"tunni hemee sai "tipani.
"Tanni tyii temu "kuu sru ii"kani chiwani"traatyi
esrku 'kan'anishi sai "tipani
srue sai tyuuw'as"tu; sai "kiwa'a'tsi
    tyuw'as"ta'a"ta.
Eume'ee tsishaatsishe hapani
heya ha'as"tiitra "ta'aisru'mane, chetsi
    tyuw'as"ta'a"ta.

The people remembered the years before,
when the land was healthy and strong.
They remembered the good years before,
when waters of the rain and melting
        snow
had filled the lake and the flowing
        streams.
They remembered the deer, antelope,
elk, and rabbits they had hunted for food,
which now were also all gone away.
Looking at dry, empty fields and gardens,
the people of Haapaahnitse were hungry.
They heard their children crying,
and they felt helpless and very sad.
Because they were no longer happy,
they grew angry and argued among
        themselves.
Without any reason except their
        helplessness,
they blamed each other for the bad times.
The close bonds of Haapaahnitse were
        breaking.

Hanu si isrka kasraiti tyu'waatyumi
"kuwasra ha'a'tsii "kunatsashe "kuu tishaatsishe.
Si rawa kasraiti tyuw'atyumi
y'uwesra kachaneu "kuu kawetau 'tsitsi
tyii 'kawaitsi tyuu"taa'a "kuu aiihonu
        chiina"ti "tisrpi.
Si "tyane "kuu kutsi tyu'waatyumi,
"kuu tyuusra "kuu retya chu'wa'waane heya
        upewi n'upesr"kune
sai chetsi ehai'ke 'kuyeiti 'teku.
Hemee ho'u tsatya tuykachani"kuyasi, sai "tipani
        "kuu tsatsinatsii tsaichu chi'wa
Hapanii'mee tyei'yayamastu.
'Iwaasi tya'a"taa 'a"ta, Hapanii'mee ty'aka,
tsatsina umaatsi tyeiyatyani "kuu tsatsina
        tiuwawiistiya.
Tsatsina tiuwawiistiyashe,
heya"ti cha'ats'ayawane "kuu cha'wainiya.
Tsatsi eutsii n'amaityu cha'wainiya. He tsatsina
        umaatsi hotiiyanishe, euu cha'wainiya.
Tsami cha'ya'maa"ti"ta, tsatsi rawa e'echa'aitrane.
Tsatsina Hapanii'mee isrka "tiu'wawitra.

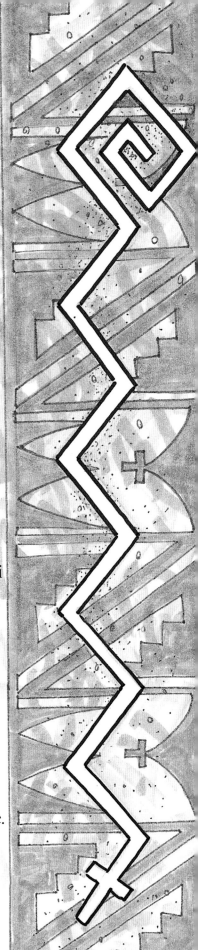

One day as the people were talking
of how poor and hard life had become,
one man said, "In the distant past,
rain and snow came across the great mountains
and the great deserts from the west."
"That is true," another man said, "but now
no longer do they cross the mountains and deserts."
They wondered why the rain and snow spirits
did not visit anymore, and they quarreled
over reasons why, although no one knew exactly why.
No one knew why life had become difficult,
and this made the people feel more hopeless.
They grew quiet for a while, deep in thought,
when out of the silence a voice softly spoke.

Hai'ku sru'e hanu chaitisha
"kuwaa tsatsina chunatsa'a'nu "kuu kuwaa chai'kishaa'wane
ishka ha'trutse e'chatsa, "Yuwee hamaashra
kaachani "kuu hawe 'tuwee 'kuti sra tseyaa'tsi
"kuu yu'ke "puniiya me'ka"tika tsatya."
Hai"ti ishka hatrutse e'chatsa, "He 'kaimatsi, esrku h'osru
tsatsina hawee 'kuuti "kuu tsatya tseyaa'tsi."
Cha'waa'tsityusta, 'tsi"kuwaaku kachani "kuu hawe mayaani
tsatsina tiu'waa"taane, srue cha'ya'tsaya'wane
euheyati, tsatsi hau tiute'emitra.
Tsatsi hau tyu"tuuni tsieu"kuwaaku chai'kishaa'wane,
mityu shrue hanu tsami ayaa'maatyusa.
Maaku tai'yatra, heme aisi cha'waa'tsityusta,
srue aisi hau maa'kume ty'a'masru.

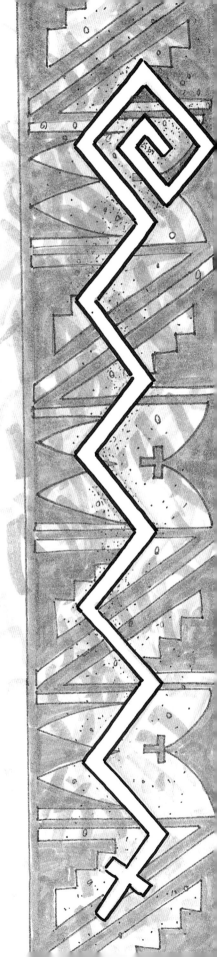

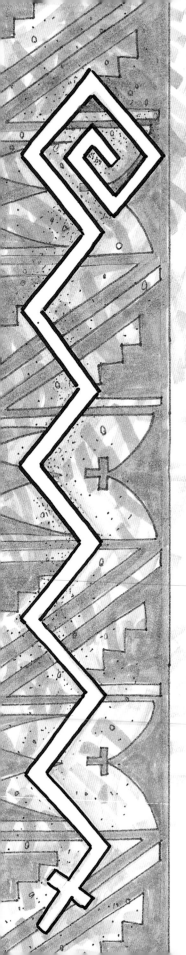

The voice was from a corner of the room,
from an old woman no one had noticed.
Slowly, she walked forward and spoke again.
"It is time to go to the west, to the home
of the Shiwana and seek their help.
It is time to go and ask them for help.
We have forgotten we must ask for help."
All the people looked closely at the old woman.
"Choose two boys," she said. "They will endure
the long, arduous journey to the Shiwana's home.
Choose them because they must go with open hearts
so they will tell the Shiwana how hard
it has become for our people and land here.
Choose them so their hearts will be open
to receive the precious gift of the Shiwana."

Aisihau shu"kuuna ty'a"pe euu ty'a'masru,
aisi 'kuuyautsa tyaku, tsatsi pu"ta hau "tiukacha.
Sraamii, sra'naya 'yaa'ni ewa'ti tsutyu, srue tsinasi tya'masru.
"Sru haa'ku ka'aitra yu'ke "puu nu"teku sutrusaa"te, aii'ka'aatru
Shiwana uumatsi nu'wawi"taa'a sutrusa.
Sru haa'ku ka'aitra eumatsi nu'wawi"taa'a sutrusa"te.
Srkuwatyumitra "kuwaa uumatsi nu'wawita'ane sutrusate."
Sai hau"pa hanu 'kuyautsa hau 'ta'akacha.
"'Etyeine"ta, "tyumii sru'yati pu"taa'ta'wane, hatruts'eme e'eniitraanu"ku'u
y'u'ke tiye, hiyaani 'kausame nu'te'eyu"kuu'u, Shiwana "ka'aatru.
Sru'yati 'niu"taa"tawe "kutrusa esr"ku niu'uhima tsiu'uma
srue Shiwana niu"pe'ene ku'unu "ku'wa
hanu "kuu ha'a'tsi chai'kishaa'wane.
Sru'yati 'niu"taa"ta "kutrusa srue
he'ya"ti iyaani naushiitsanu ku'une."

In the village of Haapaahnitse
there were two brothers: Tsaiyah-dzehshi,
who was older, and Hamahshu-dzehshi, who was younger.
First One and Next One; they were very close.
They were the boys who were chosen
to go to the west to seek the help of the Shiwana,
who were the beloved spirits of rain and snow.

Yuai Ha"paniitse ha'as"ti"tra,
tyumii sruyati chaa'yatyumushi: Tseyah Tseshi,
tsee'ya"ta, "kuu Ha'mashi Tseshe, ha'mashi ch'ani"tratyeiya.
Tseyashi 'kuu Ha'mashi tsami ty'uwiityu.
Eu sruyati 'ta"taa"tu
'yu'ke "puu nu"te'eyu tyu'u, aii Shiwana umatsi niuwi"ta'ane tyu'u
kaachani "kuu hawe Shiwana mayaani eeu "tenetsyusa.

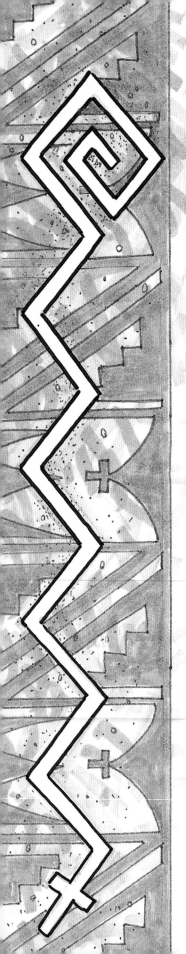

With great feeling, the women and men elders
of Haapaahnitse gave the boys their counsel.
"Beloved young men, you have been chosen
to be the ones to seek help for our people
and the land, as we have fallen on difficult
    times.
Our people are hungry, ill, and unhappy,
and all around the land is dry and barren.
Everything suffers from lack of water.
You have been chosen to take our plea
to the rain and snow Shiwana, to ask them
to visit us again with their gift of water.
Beloved young men, be thankful for being
    chosen
to carry out this task, and be thankful
for your journey to the home of the Shiwana.
Be thankful for receiving their gift from
    them."

'Kuyei "kuu umuu"titra, tsami 'amuutyusa
aii Hapaniitseme sruyati "ta'ayani "kuyanu.
"Amuu'ma sruyati, hisrueu sha"taa"ta'wane
umatsi nu'wawi"ta'a "kutru'uni hanu "ko'tsini
"kuu ha'a'tsi, ho'u tsami sai'kishawa.
Hanu "kai'ya'masta, "kuu tsai'ya'tsaa'a "kuu
    tsati tsiu'wa'wisti'ya,
"kuu sai hawe sruyana ha'a'tsii ts'i"panu "kuu
    tsatsina tsii ki'wa'tsi.
Saii'tsii 'tsitsi 'tsiu'waa'tsipu.
Hisrueu sha"taa"ta'wane ee"maani naikuutyi
    tyutruu'une
yu'ke kaachani "kuu hawee Shiwana
    ni"pe"ta'wane "kutru'u
tsinasi niu'wa"tane, kaachani 'tsitsi "tiya.
Amuu'ma sruyati, niuna'matsanu "kutru'u
    sha"ta"taa'wane
"tue'e nii"traanu tyutru'une, niu"na'matsanu
    "kutru'u
enu"te'eyu"tru'une Shiwana 'ka'atru.
Iyaani noshiitsanu "ku"truu niuna'matsanu
    "kutru'u."

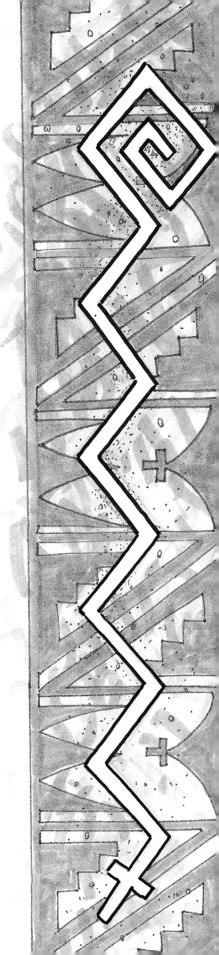

After receiving the blessings and well-wishes
of the people of Haapaahnitse,
the boys began their journey.
They had an all-important task, to help
the people and the land, and they must do all
they could to take word to the Shiwana in the west.
Tsaiyah-dzehshi and Hamahshu-dzehshi must do
their best so the Shiwana of the rain and snow
would bring the gift of life to Haapaahnitse.

Srusai utsa'anikuya cho'shiitsanu
Ha"pani'meesi
sruyati srue "te'eyu.
Umaatsi tii'itranu 'kasrkatsityume
hanu "kuu ha'a'tsi "kau'tsini, tsiihai"ti "ka'tsipatyau
'maani naikutyi tyu'u yu'ke "puu Shiwana 'ka'atru.
Tseya tseshi "kuu Hamashi tseshi se"katse
hatrutseme e'enii"traanu tyu'u heeya Shiwana kaachani "kuu hawe
Ha"paniitse iyaani hawe 'neiku'mi 'ta'a'mane.

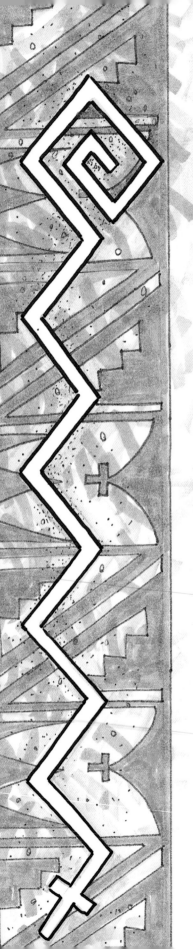

It was a long and difficult journey
the boys had to travel. There were mountains
with high red peaks they had to climb.
There were dangerous, slippery rock places
and deep canyons they had to climb into and out of.
After the mountains, there was a vast desert
where everything was dry and dead in the hot sun.

Tiye"ta "kuu hiyaani tsatsi rawa"ta
ewa sruyati se"katse "te'eyu, aii 'kuuti
ku"kani tiyetyi s'tu'kutsi eetyii sekatse tya'aiya.
Aii piirii"kanu 'yauni"ta, tsatsi rawa"ta
"kuu nukatsa chinaya nutya'aya "kuu sityii tya'aya
Saii 'kuuti tyumu, aii mee'ka"tika tsatya"ta
aii 'kananii"ta saitsi'ai "tepani "kuu ch'u'stunu.

Everywhere the boys looked, nothing was alive:
no plants, no animals, not even tiny insects.
The boys were more determined than ever
to cross the next range of tall, black mountains,
because behind those mountains they were sure
they would arrive at the home of the Shiwana.
But when they climbed the mountains,
they nearly froze from the ferocious winds
blowing constantly, and they had to stop.
However, slowly and courageously inching their way
up and down the treacherous mountain cliffs,
First One and Next One did not stop,
and at last they had crossed the mountains.

Sruyati saii hawee tyukachanu, tsatsitsii chaa'yune:
tsatsitsii 'chiwa, tsatsitsii 'kuyeiti "tiya, tsatsitsii shchari "tiya.
Sruyati simuchu "taa'aitra
muna'kani 'kuuti niumu tyu'une,
"tinaitrane aiikaatya 'kuuti
Shiwana 'achini hau'u nu"tra'a'tsi tyu'une.
Esr"kusru 'kuuti tyii tya'aiyani
maii chame"tunu tsami tsishatsi tyuyu"tawa
'tsi'kaatsi tyuyu"tawa, maii chutya'tsimu.
Esr"kusru hatrutsemee sraamii sran'a'ya chutsitsuutsu "taanu
'kamatsaisru 'kuuti tyii tya'aya "kuu nutya'aya,
Tseyashi "kuu Hamashi tsatsi chutya'tsimu
srue hai'ku 'kuuti tyuu'mu.

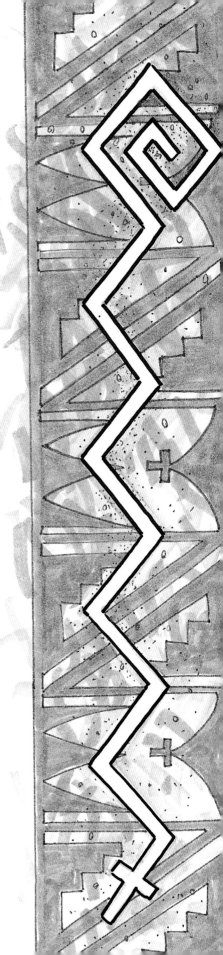

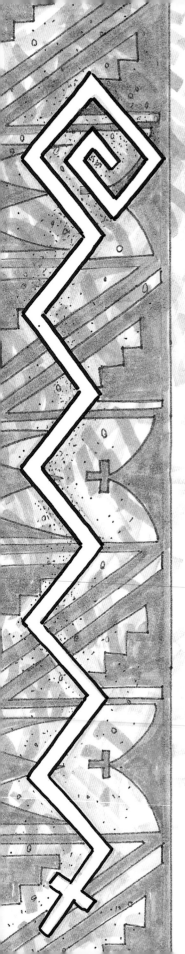

When at last the boys got through boulders
at the foot of the mountains,
they were stopped by a deep chasm.
The chasm was a canyon filled with volcanic lava
that roared and surged like a fiery river;
from the molten stone fiercely leaped hot flames.
An acrid and sour odor of sulphur rose from it,
and waves of heat drove the boys backward.
First One and his younger brother, Next One,
wondered how to cross the canyon of fire.
First One spoke then. He said, "We must leap
across this canyon of lava, younger brother.

Srue hai'ku sruyati "tusr"kutsichi yauni tya'ai'yatyu
'kuuti nutsiyaa
nu"katsa chinaya "titya'tsi'manu.
Nu"katsa chinaya haa'kaani"ti tyuu'ta
tsami tyush'chetsi"ta "kuu 'tsitsi'mee tsishatsi "tisr"pii'ya'a"ta;
yauni haa'kaani tsami shcha'ushch'autya.
Tsami 'kawasta aremee "pusrutya,
"kuu 'chash'chutru srue katyama sruyati sa"te'eyu.
Tseyashi "kuu mu"tetsa 'katyumu, Hamashi
Ch'u'tsityustaanu "kuwa chinaya tsayacho "kuya niumutyu'une.
Srue Tseyashi tya'masru. E'chatsa, "Se"katse n'u"tuutsaanusutru'u
'yu'kee ha'kaani chinaya, mu"tetsa satyuu'mu.

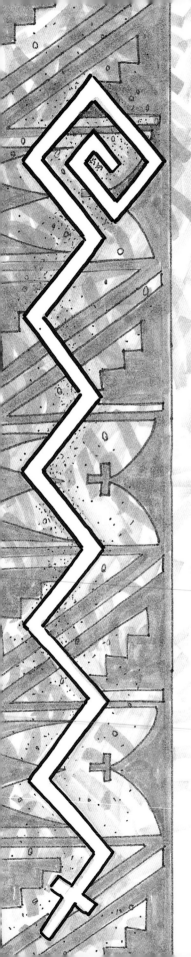

Gather all the strength and courage of your heart
and leap as hard and as high as you can.
We must have the belief to leap across.
We are on a task to help our people and our land."
With those words, First One gave a great yell
and leaped to the far side of the canyon.
He landed on safe ground from where he could see
the horizon of tall trees where the Shiwana lived.

Saiie shi'shaatsishe "kuu sra'winasrkasi hatstrume
tsishatsi tiyeetyi n'u"tuutsasru.
Niu'u-hima sr"k'u'um'a 'i"te niumu sutru'une
sr'kwii'itranu hanu "kuu ha'a'tsi nei'wamatsani'" taa."
Heme sai 'chatsa'ane, Tseyashi 'ayame "taish'chautsa
'chu"tuutsa yu'ke 'isr"kaya chinaya"ti.
Aii rawa nutsatya "tesru nuchucha, aiinusitya"pe tyukacha
sr"pu"tii hii"tra'ai chiwa euaii Shiwana tya'aa"tru.

Next One felt searing heat from the molten lava.
The other side of the canyon was very far.
The chasm was wide, and the glowing lava in it
roared fiercely, like an angry ancient monster.
He grew frightened, and he was hesitant to leap.
He looked at the fiery chasm and at his brother
on the other side, then at the ground at his feet.
He wanted to run and leap over the fiery lava,
but his fear froze him to the ground.
Next One began to cry. He lacked the courage
to cross the volcanic chasm,
and he felt tears begin to fill his eyes.

Tsami ha'kaani 'chash'chuutru Hamashi 'chastitsina.
Yu'wisa chinaaya "tyiye'e"ta.
Chinaya mee'ka"titya "kuu aiinu haa'kaani tyeitra
tsaami tyuush'chetsa 'yue hi"kaantime.
Tsatsi Hamashi etyu nu"tuutsatyune "kuu sru'e chu"putsa.
Ho'u ha'kaani chinaya "kuu 'katyumu tyukacha,
"yu'wisa aiisi tyuchani, srue haunu nutsatya kasti tyu"kacha.
'Kai'ka nitrutsatyu "kuu n'u"tuutsatyu
esrku mityu chu"putsau "tuu aiisi me"tiitra.
Srue Hamashi chatikuya; tsatsi hatrutseme e'etii"tra
ha"kaani chinaya eniumu'tyune,
srue tsinasi 'chan'asr"pe'e'yu'tsi.

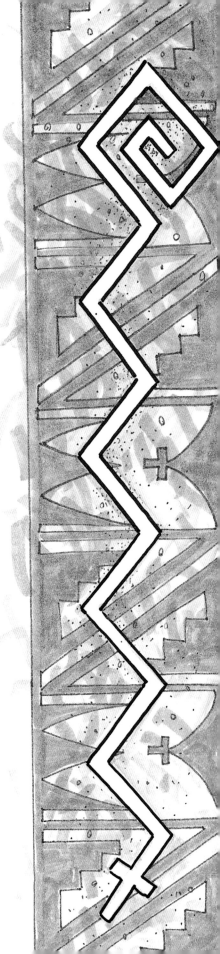

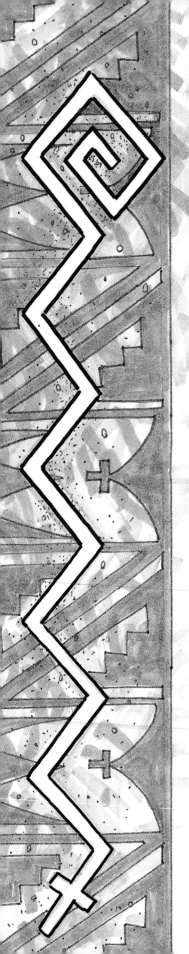

First One saw that his brother was frightened.
He loved him and wanted to encourage him.
First One called as loudly as he could,
"Beloved brother, have courage. Hahtruudzaimeh!
We must go on. The Shiwana live not far away."
Although he called loudly, his words were lost
in the roar of the flowing river of lava,
and Next One could not hear what he said.
The boys had to go on; they had been sent
to take word to the Shiwana; they were to help
the people and the land; they must go on.

Tseyashi 'katyumu tyukacha ch'u"putsane.
Tseyashi 'katyumu tyuu'tsimi, hatrutseme 'niya'nikuyatyu.
Tyeyashi ayaame "taish'chautsa,
"Satyumu sro'tsimi, hatrutseme e'enitrasru. Hatrutseme!
'Tsi'kaa'tsi nu"te'e'ya'"ta su"tru'u. Tsatsi tiiye Shiwana ka'atru."
Ayaame "taish'chautsa, esr"ku tsatsi tyii 'tetramu
tsami ha'kaaka chiina 'cha'tsaisrka,
tsatsi 'i"te Hamashi chaka "k'wi Tseyashi 'chatsa'ane.
Sekatse sruyati nu"te'e'ya'a"ta tyu'u; "tii'itranu
'maani naikuutyityu'u 'yu'ke Shiwana"ti' nei'; wa'maatsanityu'u
hanu "kuu ha'a'tsii; 'tsi'kaa'tsi nu"te'e'ya'a"ta tyu'u.

But Next One was helpless with fear.
He looked at his brother in the distance again,
trying very hard to hear his brother's words.
Next One at last heard First One holler.
Over the loud roaring of the fiery river,
he heard his brother shout, "Look back!
Look behind you!" What was he to see behind him?
But, following his brother's bidding,
Next One saw someone coming down the mountain.

Esrku Hamashi tsatsi 'i"te "tiu'witra, tsami ch'u"putsa;
Hamashi 'katyumu hautyukacha, tiyesi tyuchani.
Chi"paitsa nekaa"kune, "k'wi 'katyumu 'chatsa'ane,
hai'kusru Hamashi chaka Tseyashi "taiishchautsani.
Tsami ha'kaaka chiina 'cha'tsaisrkate,
esrku chaka 'katyumu "taish'chautsani, ""Katyama 'ika.
Katyama 'ika." Tsii aii kaatya niukachatyu?
Srue katyama "tika, 'yuee "katyumu e"tii'yanikuyani,
Hamashi tyukacha, haweenu 'kutinuhau 'chanitratyeiya.

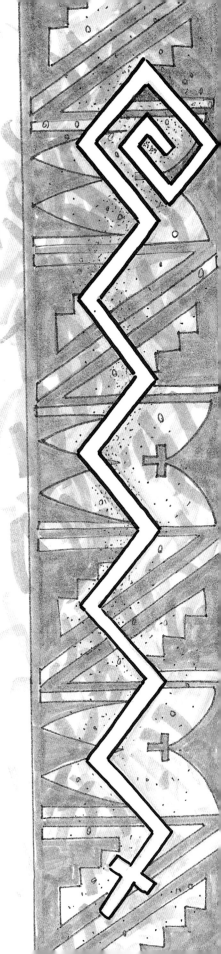

Slowly, carefully, the person came toward him,
and toward the dangerous chasm of lava!
Wiping away his tears, Next One saw it was a woman,
an old woman who felt her way among the boulders.
The white-haired woman seemed not to see
the danger before her, and Next One realized
she was blind! She was headed for the chasm!
Instinctively, not thinking of anything else,
he leaped forward and spoke to the old woman.
"Grandmother, please, you must stop.
For the sake of your life, I beg you,
you must stop. There is danger ahead!"

Sraami, sraanaya, aii hou "tiu'wa'tsi.
Ewa"ti ha'kaani chinaya 'chanitratyeiya!
'Kan'asrpe'e'yu cha'o'kaya Hamashi 'ku'witsa tyukacha,
'ku'yotsa ha'we me'kache yaunishi cha'o"taanikyua.
"Kashe kuse'eni 'kuyautsa "tuutsi tsatsi tyukacha
aii 'yani tsatsi rawa "ta'ane, srue Hamashi tiu"te'emitra
tsatsi "tiikasti! Ha'kaani chinaya ewa"ti 'chanitratyeiya!
Tsanae'etyune,
aii 'yani chu"tuutsa srue 'kuyautsa "tatisha.
"Sa"tao, naishetse, "paa trutya'tsi'i.
Naniyaanisrune, eu"tu sra'yani"kuya,
"paatrutya'tsi'i. Tsatsi aii 'yani rawats'a!"

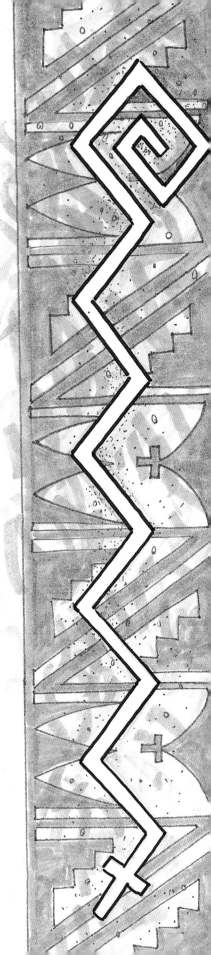

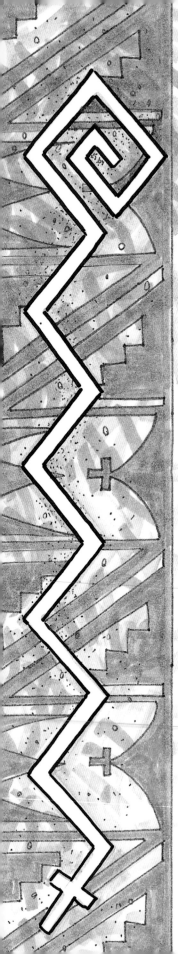

The old woman was very tiny,
and when Next One looked closely at her,
she looked like what he had heard
the Spider Grandmother looked like.
With her white-turned eyes, she turned
    to him
and said, "Thank you, beloved grandson,
for warning me." And then sensing
his tears and sadness, she kindly asked,
"Why have you been crying, Grandson?"
Although he did not want to at first,
Next One said, "I've been unable to leap
across the canyon of molten lava.
My brother and I were sent to summon
the Shiwana to help our land and people.
I am afraid, and now I cannot cross the
    canyon,
and I will not be able to complete my
    task."
Gently the woman said, "Thank you,
    Grandson,
for looking back and seeing me.
You saw I am blind and you helped me.
It's good too you have told me your fear.
I shall help you in turn, beloved grandson.
You have an important task you must
    complete."

'Kuyautsa tsaami rutishi
srue Hamashi hau'u sraami tyukacha,
'yu cha"kaane
"Tao 'Kamasrka euu etyukacha.
Kashe tyinamityi "tikani "kuya hau'u
    Hamashi tyukacha
srue e"tatsi"kuya, "Amuu sa"paa"pa, nai'tra
tyumaasrutsani." Srue metsii cha'autyu"ko
'chan'asrpe'e'yutsi "kuu tsatsi tiuwiistiyane,
    amuume tyupee"ta,
"Tsii"ku"waaku sra"tikuyasi, sa"paa"pa?"
Tsatsi 'kaii"ka tse'ya'ma etyu, esrku,
Hamashi e'chatsa, "Tsatsi 'i"te sr"ku"tuutsa
ha'kee ha'kaani chinaya.
Satyumu hawe sr'ka'a"ku'yani u'wa"peutsa
Shiwana etse ha'a'tsi "kuu hanu
    nei'wamaatsani"kusa.
Su"putsa, tsatsi 'i"te chinaya shchiyatyu
tsatsi 'i"te sr'kwii'itrane ni'no"tasr'ku."
Amuume e'chatsa, "Nai'tra, sa"paa"pa,
katyama shi"kaane "kuu tyuukachane.
Tyukacha tsatsi tu"tiish"kane srue
    tyumatsani.
Rawa e'eshii"tra tyu"pe'eni he"tru"puutsane.
Amuuma sa"paa"pa, che'yuna niu'matsanis-
    ro'ma,
'kaasrkatsityume sra'ai"kuu'ya'a"ta se"kaatse
    ni'no"tasru."

The old woman untied a flowered
    handkerchief
she had, and from it she took a tiny stone.
She held it up between her long, thin fingers.
She said to Next One, "Take this stone.
Tie it to your arrow," and she gave it to him.
"Then put the arrow to your bow and pull it
with all your strength and let it fly."
Next One did as he was told, tied the stone
to the arrow with sinew, fit it to his bow,
and pulled the bowstring with all
    his might.

'Ku'witsa 'kawaisutru 'paani tyusr"pu"tuwa
aiisi rusrkishi yauni tyu"ku.
Tyii yauni "ti"taiku, me'tsu"tru 'kamaa"pu"ti.
Srue Hamashi e"tatsi"kuya, ""Tu yauni
    'chu"taiku.
'Kutra is"tuwa aii nipashchasru," srue yauni
    "tiu"ti.
"Srue is"tuwa 'wish'cha'kati aii'ni"panai'isru
    srue niunutsasru
saiie shishaatsishe, srue 'naa"tuwisru."
Ha'mashi e'e"tii"tra "kuwa 'ta'ayani "kuya
    sinani"ti yauni "ti"pashcha
is"tu'wa"ti, srue is"tu'wa 'wish'cha"ka
    aii"ti"panai'i,
srue saiie tishaatsishe hii'kashchi "ku'kumiina
    tyunutsa.

When he let it go, the arrow sang through the air.
It arced far and high over the fiery lava.
And as the arrow soared in its flight,
in the path it took there formed a rainbow.
It was a rainbow road, a good rainbow road.

In the brilliant yet soft colors of light—
yellow, blue, red, all the colors of sky and land,
all the colors of plant and animal life—
the rainbow was a wonderful, beautiful sight.
Holding his bow, Next One stood quietly in awe
until the woman said, "You must climb on the rainbow now, Grandson. You must go
on with your journey to meet the Shiwana."

Srue 'cha"tyuwiine, is"tu'wa
  ch'ai-tsa'a'tsime ch'u'yu"ta.
Is"tu'wa tiiyeetyi uraasr"pa cha'aitra
  ha'kaani chinaya"ti.
Srue is"tu'wa tyi chi'ya'a"tanu
'kashtyaa'tsi hawe echa'aitra.
Kashtyaa'tsi hiyaani eu"ta, rawaa"ta
  'kashtyaa'
  tsi hiyaawa.

Tsami stemimiitya "kuu tsinamii tsatsi
  stemimiitya–
'kuuchini, 'kwisr"kuni, ku"kani, saieu
  hena"ti kuu ha'a'tsi 'chawaisutru

saii "ki'wa'tsi "kuu 'kuyei"ti hiya'kaatsi
  'cha'waisutru–
'kashtyaa'tsi tsami 'kauname,
  "kwi'na'ma"te.
Aiisi Ha'mashi 'wish'chaa'ka
  cha'aikuuya, "tuu aiisi
  maa"ku 'me"titra
srue 'ku'witsa "tyamasru, "Se"katse
  tyiini'yasru
'kashtyaa'tsishi, sa"paa"pa. Se"katse
  tsunesru
aii Shiwana ni'wa"tai'isru."

The boy turned once more to look back
at the steep and rugged mountains
and the hot, dry deserts he and First One
had traveled, and he thought of the people
and the land far beyond the deserts
and mountains who needed help.
And he looked toward the west,
where the Shiwana lived at the horizon.
He turned to the old woman then and said,
"Thank you for helping me, beloved grandmother,
so that I may help the people and the land.
I will always remember you."
Hamahshu-dzehshi climbed onto the rainbow road
and quickly ran on the road high above
the canyon of fiery lava and joined his brother,
Tsaiyah-dzehshi, and together they journeyed
to take the plea of help to the Shiwana
for their beloved people and land.

Mu"tetsa tsinasi kaytyama "tika, tsinasi
    tyukacha
nukatsa, 'kamatsasru 'kuuti
"kuu 'tsi"pani, 'kanani tsatya ee Tseyashi
"te'e'yune, sruesi hanu tyuwatyu'mi
"kuu ha'a'tsi 'yuhaa"ti tsatya
"kuu 'kuti umaatsi tiu'tsipa"te.
Srue "punami ewa "tika
'yuai usra"tra nu'tsi'yaa'
    tsi'ma aii Shiwana tya'atru.
Hau'u 'kuwitsa tyukacha,
    srue e"tatsi"kuya,
"Amuu sa"ta'o, wu'e tyumatsani.

He'yashi hanu "kuu ha'a'tsii nei'wamatsanisi.
Sru hai'kumii niutyumi srau'ma."
Ha'mashi tseshe 'kashtyaa'tsi hiyaani tyii
    tyu'ya
srue eetyii hiyaani sh'chatru chitrutsa, tiyeetyii
ha'kaani chinaya, srue aii 'katyumu sa'
    chayeityamu,
Tseyaa tseshi, srue isr"kawa e"te'eyu
"tii'itrane umaatsi yu'ke Shiwana"ti
he'ya amuu hanu "kuu ha'a'tsi kau'tsini.

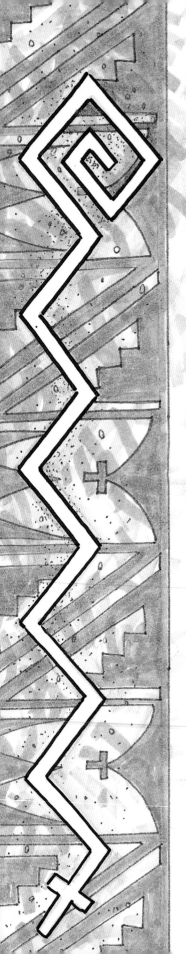

Yes, it is very important to look back upon the sacred knowledge
so that we may live by it in a good and healthy way.

*Hautyi 'kaasrka 'ka'yatuuni niukachane sutrusa, 'kaasrkatsityume eutsa
srue heya"ti 'kauname sr'katru'tsini nu"te'esutrusa.*

El Buen Camino
DEL ARCO IRIS

Simon J. Ortiz

Dedicado a Sara, para que ella y todos los otros niños del mundo puedan andar siempre por buenos caminos. También a mis nietas: Krista, Desirray, Monique, Tayo, and Chayson.

En este momento, que abarca más de cuatrocientos años desde el comienzo de la colonización de nuestros pueblos indígenas por Europa, este cuento es, en particular, para nuestra gente que se mantuvo siempre como parte de la misma tierra, nuestra cultura y la comunidad. Sí, siempre la tierra, la cultura y la comunidad; siempre la gente alimentada de amor, compasión, rezo, esperanza, valentía y humildad; siempre la creencia en nuestra soberanía sagrada; siempre la sana creencia en nosotros mismos.

Debemos ver siempre hacia nuestro pasado y reconocer la vía buena que nuestra gente ha caminado. Debemos acudir siempre al conocimiento sagrado que ha sustentado a nuestra gente. No solamente debemos recordar, sino también debemos vivir las formas saludables, la vía buena de la cultura y la tradición. De esta manera, nosotros siempre continuaremos siendo gente fuerte y saludable.

Hace muchos, pero muchos años,
existía un pueblo al pie de la montaña Haapaahni Quuti.
La montaña se llamaba así, Haapaahni,
por los árboles de roble que allí crecían.
Y por eso el pueblo fue llamado así
Haapaahnitse, el Lugar de los Robles.
Cerca de Haapaahnitse, había un lago
y en este lago se desembocaba un arroyo.
Pero ahora, ya no existe el lago,
y el arroyo tambien dejó de fluir;
pues se habían secado hace ya muchos años.
Aún ahora, todavía estan secos porque por muchos años
no ha llovido ni ha caído nieve por aquí.

La gente de Haapaahnitse
había cultivado maíz, calabazas, frijoles y chile
en las tierras a orillas del lago,
y habían regado sus cultivos
con las aguas del arroyo cuando fluía.
Nada les faltaba,
pues tenían muchas cosas que comer
y estaban felices.
Y entonces sucedió que por mucho, mucho tiempo, la lluvia y la nieve
no llegaron y por eso la tierra se secó.
Cuando la gente sembraba los granos de maíz,
las plantas crecían altas y luego se secaban.
Las calabazas brotaban y extendían sus bejucos
pero se marchitaban bajo el sol caliente
y pronto se morían; todas las planta se morían.
Hasta los fuertes y robustos árboles de roble,
cuyo nombre llevaba el pueblo, se morían.

La gente se acordaba de los años anteriores
cuando la tierra era fértil y productiva.
La gente se acordaba de los buenos años que habían pasado,

cuando las aguas de la lluvia y de la nieve derritida,
llenaban el lago y el pequeño arroyo.
La gente se acordaba de los venados, los antílopes,
el alce y los conejos que cazaban para comer,
los cuales ahora también habían desaparecido.
Mirando a los campos y jardines secos y vacíos,
la gente de Haapaahnitse sintió el hambre.
Escuchaban las quejas y los gemidos de sus hijos
y se sentían indefensos y muy tristes.
En estas condiciones ya no estaban felices
y comenzaron a enojarse y a pelearse entre ellos mismos.
Sin ninguna razón, excepto por la desgracia que vivían,
se acusaban los unos a los otros por el mal tiempo.
Así los íntimos lazos que unían a la gente de Haapaahnitse se
    desvanecieron.

Cierto día, mientras al gente hablaba
de cómo se había hecho difícil y dura la vida,
uno de los hombres dijo, "En tiempos pasados,
la lluvia y la nieve venían y cruzaban las grandes montañas
y los grandes desiertos en el occidente".
"Es cierto", dijo otro hombre, "pero ahora
ya no pasan y cruzan las montañas y los desiertos".
Ellos se preguntaban por qué los espíritus de la lluvia y de la nieve
ya no los visitaban como antes, y se peleaban
por dar explicaciones, aunque nadie sabía exactamente por qué.
Nadie sabía por qué la vida se había vuelto tan difícil
y esto les hacía sentir mas desdichados.
Se calmaron por un rato y meditaron;
luego una voz rompió el silencio y habló suavemente.
La voz surgió en una esquina del espacio,
la cual provenía de una anciana que nadie había notado antes.
Lentamente, la anciana avanzó y habló de nuevo.
"Es tiempo de ir al occidente, a la casa

de los Shiwana y pedirles ayuda.
Es el tiempo oportuno para ir a pedirles ayuda.
Nos hemos olvidado que debemos pedir ayuda".
Toda la gente se acercó a mirar a la anciana.
"Elijan a dos jóvenes", dijo ella. "Ellos podrán resistir
el largo y arduo camino hacia la casa de los Shiwana.
Elíjanlos, porque tendrán que ir con un corazón brillante
a decirles a los Shiwana de lo difícil
que se ha vuelto aquí la vida para la gente y la misma tierra.
Elíjanlos para que sus corazones esten preparados
para recibir el precioso regalo de los Shiwana".

En el pueblo de Haapaahnitse
habían dos hermanos: Tsaiyah-dzehshi,
que era el hermano mayor, y Hamahshu-dzehshi, el menor.
El-que-es-Primero y El-que-es-Segundo—se querían mucho.
Estos fueron los muchachos elegidos
para ir al occidente a pedir la ayuda de los Shiwana,
que eran los adorados espíritus de la lluvia y de la nieve.
Con gran sentimiento, las mujeres y hombres mayores
de Haapaahnitse dieron sus consejos a los muchachos.
"Queridos muchachos, ustedes han sido escogidos
para ir a buscar la ayuda para nuestra gente
y para la tierra, pues hemos caído en tiempos difíciles.
Nuestra gente está hambrienta, enferma y triste,
y en todas partes la tierra está seca y estéril.
Todas las cosas sufren por la falta de agua.
Ustedes han sido escogidos para llevar nuestra súplica
a los Shiwana, espíritus de la lluvia y de la nieve; y pedirles
que nos visiten de nuevo con su regalo de agua.
Queridos jóvenes, sean agradecidos por haber sido escogidos
para realizar este trabajo, y sean agradecidos
por su viaje a la casa de los Shiwana.
Sean agradecidos al recibir el regalo de ellos".

Después de recibir las bendiciones y los buenos deseos
de la gente de Haapaahnitse,
los muchachos comenzaron su viaje.
Ellos iban en una faena de mayor importancia: ayudar
a la gente y a la tierra, y tenían que hacer todo lo posible
para llevar el mensaje a los Shiwana en el occidente.
Tsaiyah-dzehshi y Hamahshu-dzehshi tenían que hacer
todo lo posible para que los Shiwana de la lluvia y de la nieve
trajeran el regalo de vida a la gente de Haapaahnitse.

Este era un camino largo y muy difícil
que los muchachos tenían que realizar, así como las montañas
con altos, rojos picachos que tenían que ascender.
Habían lugares peligrosos de rocas resbaladizas
y barrancos profundos donde tenían que bajar y subir.
Pasando las montañas, había un desierto vasto
donde todo estaba seco y muerto por el calor del sol.
Dondequiera que veían, nada encontraban con vida:
ni plantas, ni animales, ni siquiera pequeños insectos.
Los muchachos estaban aún más decididos,
para cruzar otra cadena de montañas negras y altas,
porque detrás de esas montañas ellos estaban seguros
que encontrarían la casa de los Shiwana.
Pero cuando ascendieron las montañas,
casi se congelaron por los vientos feroces
que soplaban constantemente, de manera que tuvieron que parar.
Así se acercaban lentamente y con valor,
por arriba y por abajo de los picos traicioneros y montañosos
"El-que-es-Primero" y "El-que-es-Segundo", no se detuvieron
y por fin cruzaron las montañas.

Cuando por fin los muchachos pasaron las grandes rocas
al pie de las montañas,
otro abismo profundo los detuvo.

El abismo era un hueco lleno de lava volcánica
que rugía y surgía como un río incandecente;
y de las piedras derritidas saltaban ferozes llamas candentes.
Un fuerte hedor de azufre putrefacto salía del fondo
y unas olas de calor empujaron a los muchachos hacia atrás.
El-que-es-Primero y su hermano menor, El-que-es-Segundo,
se pusieron a pensar en cómo cruzar el abismo de fuego.
El-que-es-Primero habló y dijo: "Debemos lanzarnos sobre
este abismo lleno de lava, hermano menor.
Cobra toda la fuerza y valentía de tu corazón y
salta lo más fuerte y alto que puedes.
Debemos tener la fe para saltar sobre este abismo;
pues estamos en una tarea para nuestra gente y nuestra tierra".
Con esas palabras, El-que-es-Primero gritó con todas sus fuerzas
y saltó hasta llegar al otro lado del abismo.
El había logrado llegar a un lugar seguro desde donde podía ver
un horizonte de grandes árboles donde vivían los Shiwana.

El-que-es-Segundo sintió el terrible calor de la lava ardiente.
La otra orilla del abismo estaba demasiado lejos.
El abismo era ancho y la lava luminosa en el fondo
rugía ferozmente como un antiguo monstruo temible.
El muchacho vaciló en saltar y comenzó a asustarse.
Miraba la lava rugiente y a su hermano
en el otro lado, luego miraba el suelo bajo sus pies.
El quería correr y saltar sobre la lava hirviente
pero el miedo lo paralizó sobre el suelo.
El-que-es-Segundo empezó a llorar. No tenía el valor
para saltar sobre el abismo de lava,
y entonces sus ojos comenzaron a llenarse de lágrimas.

El-que-es-Primero se dio cuenta de que su hermano estaba
    asustado.
El quería a su hermano y trató de animarlo.

El-que-es-Primero llamó en alta voz,
"Querido hermano, ten valor. ¡Hahtruudzaimeh!
Debemos seguir adelante. Los Shiwana no viven lejos de aquí".
A pesar de sus gritos, sus palabras se perdieron
entre el rugir del río de lava ardiente,
de manera que El-que-es-Segundo no pudo oír nada.
Los muchachos tenían que continuar el viaje, habían sido enviados
a llevar el mensaje a los Shiwana; tenían que ayudar
a la gente y a la tierra; tenían que seguir adelante;
pero El-que-es-Segundo estaba paralizado por el miedo.
Una vez más, a lo lejos divisó a su hermano
e hizo el esfuerzo de captar lo que su hermano le decía.
El-que-es-Segundo al fin escuchó el grito de su hermano.
Sobre el bullicioso rugir del río de lava
oyó a su hermano gritar, "Mira atrás.
Mira atrás de ti". ¿Qué era lo que el tenía que ver allí atrás?
Siguiendo lo que su hermano le decía,
El-que-es-Segundo se volteó a alguien que bajaba de la montaña.

Despacio, cuidadosamente, la persona se le acercó a él.
Aquel persona se fue acercando al gran abismo de lava.
Limpiándose las lágrimas, El-que-es Segundo vio que era
      una mujer, una anciana que tanteaba su camino por las grandes rocas.
La mujer de pelo blanco parecía no ver el peligro en su camino,
entonces, El-que-es-Segundo se dio cuenta de
que la anciana era ciega. ¡Estaba encaminandose al abismo!
      Instintivamente, y sin pensar en nada,
él saltó hacia adelante y le habló a la anciana.
"¡Abuela, por favor debe detenerse.
Por su propia vida, le suplico
que pare. Hay un gran peligro adelante!"

La anciana era muy pequeña
y cuando El-que-es-Segundo la miró de cerca,
ella se parecía a la que señalaban como la Abuela-Araña.

Con sus ojos blanqueados, ella volteó hacia él
y le dijo, "Muchas gracias mi querido nieto
por alertarme del peligro". Y dándose cuenta
de sus lágrimas y tristeza, ella le dijo amablemente,
"¿Por qué has estado llorando, querido nieto?"
Aunque al principio no quería decir nada,
El-que-es-Segundo dijo, "No he podido saltar
a través de este abismo de lava ardiente.
Mi hermano y yo fuimos enviados a pedir ayuda
a los Shiwana para asistir a nuestra tierra y a nuestra gente.
Pero tengo miedo, ahora no puedo cruzar el abismo
y no podré realizar mi faena".
Serenamente la anciana dijo, "Gracias, mi nieto,
por voltear hacia atrás y verme.
Te diste cuenta que yo era ciega y me ayudaste.
También es bueno que me hayas contado de tu temor.
Por esta razón, te voy a ayudar, mi nieto querido,
vas a una misión importante y la tienes que terminar".

La anciana desató un pañuelo floreado
que ella tenía y del pañuelo sacó una piedra pequeña.
La elevó entre sus largos y delgados dedos.
Luego, le dijo a El-que-es-Segundo,
"Toma esta piedra y amárrala a tu flecha". Y se la regaló.
"Ahora, fija la flecha en tu arco, estírala
con todas tus fuerzas y déjala volar".
El-que-es-Segundo siguió las instrucciones.
Amarró la piedra a su flecha y la ajustó al arco;
luego estiró la cuerda del arco con toda su fuerza.
Al dispararla, la flecha voló por el aire,
dibujando un arco sobre la lava candente.
Mientras la flecha volaba por el aire,
el camino que fue trazando se convirtió en un arco iris.
Era un camino de colores, un camino bueno de arco iris.

Eran los brillantes y a la vez, suaves colores de la luz—
amarillo, azul, rojo; todos los colores del cielo y de la tierra,
todos los colores de las plantas y de los animales—
el arco iris estaba allí como una visión preciosa.
Con el arco en la mano, El-que-es-Segundo se quedó sorprendido,
       hasta que la anciana dijo, "Ahora debes subirte
al arco iris, mi nieto. Tienes que seguir
tu camino para ir a conocer a los Shiwana".
El muchacho dio vuelta para ver una vez más hacia atrás
las montañas escarpadas y altas,
y los desiertos secos y quemantes que el y El-que-es-Primero
ya habían caminado. Se acordó de la gente
y de las tierras lejanas que necesitaban ayuda,
mas allá de los desiertos y las montañas.
Entonces, el miró hacia el occidente
donde los Shiwana vivían allá en el horizonte.
Se dirigió a la anciana y le dijo,
"Gracias por ayudarme, querida abuela,
para que yo pueda asistir a la gente y a la tierra.
Yo siempre te recordaré".
Hamahshu-dzehshi se subió al camino de arco iris
y rápidamente corrió sobre ese camino arqueado
sobre el abismo de lava ardiente y se reunió con su hermano
Tsaiyah-dzehshi; y juntos viajaron
Llevando la petición de ayuda a los Shiwana
para ayudar a su gente y a su tierra que tanto amaban.

Sí, es muy importante regresar al conocimiento sagrado, de manera que podamos vivir bajo su luz y en un camino bueno y saludable.

Traducción de Víctor D. Montejo

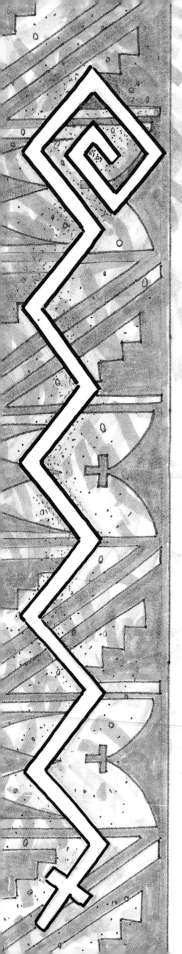

ABOUT THIS BOOK

THE GOOD RAINBOW ROAD is not a traditional Native American story. It is not a story that is told in any Native cultural community. It is not traditional in any technical meaning of the word, because the story is a contemporary creative work by the Native author who wrote it. However, it contains elements of traditional storytelling. These elements are common to and recognizable by the universal human cultural community no matter the ethnic identity or geographic locale. One of those elements is a belief in the power of language and memory. As a community, we have languages with which to communicate and relate to each other as people and to the world around us, and we have had an all-abiding memory since the beginning of time and since human culture became aware of Existence within it. *The Good Rainbow Road* is located in the Native American (or Indian) culturally conscious world, but it is not limited to that world. Even considering humankind's many ethnic differences, we are all part of each other as people and all the rest of Creation. Our stories join us together. This, I believe, is the basis of *The Good Rainbow Road*.

There has been a collaborative effort to bring the story out as a book. After writing it about ten years ago, I thought it would become another children's book, somewhat like the three I've done previously. Several years ago, I showed the story to Beverly Slapin, executive director of Oyate, who had asked me what I was currently writing. She really liked the story and proposed a dimension I had previously given brief thought to: a trilingual story and book—Indian (or Native American), English, and Spanish. Beverly introduced me to Michael Lacapa—a talented Hopi Tewa–White Mountain Apache artist and children's book author—and began fundraising, and we began the process of having the story published as a trilingual book for young people.

Michael Lacapa added an important visual dimension to the story. Since stories are abstract language events envisioned in concrete visual terms by the cultural imagination, in a sense the abstract concepts of verbal language can only be communicated by visual artwork. Victor Montejo, a Mayan who is writer, poet, and anthropologist, did the Spanish language translation of the story I had written in English. I was happy Professor Montejo could do it because I wanted a translation into Spanish by a Native-language speaker who knew at firsthand pertinent matters that have bearing on Spanish language use by Native people in the Americas.

In considering Indigenous language translation, I had literally hundreds of Native languages to choose from, all of them important to consider since the first languages of the Americas are Indian or Native American. But I wanted a language from the cultural region I am most familiar with, the region of the Americas known as the American Southwest since I am a native of Acoma Pueblo in New Mexico. I preferred the primary language to be Keres because it is the native Acoma language and the language I knew and spoke before I learned English in school. I was aware that there are differing schools of thought on Keres language use, literacy, teaching, and related matters. And I knew of past and present efforts to ensure that Native languages, at Acoma and elsewhere, continue to be a part of Native American cultural life. Discussions with some Acoma language speakers who are formally trained Keres linguists made me aware of a concern with Keres language teaching. These people assert—correctly so, to some degree—that Keres should be taught and learned as a spoken language, not via writing. I decided upon a translation by a Keres language consultant, a native speaker from a sister Keres-speaking Pueblo. Keres is the parent language known and spoken by the Pueblos of Acoma, Laguna, Santo Domingo, Cochiti, San Felipe, Santa Ana, and Zia, but there are speaking differences or dialects particular to each community locale. Although generally categorized into Eastern and Western Keres, Keres writing differs from Pueblo to Pueblo because of the dialects, which are differentiated by diacritical marks and symbols. My insistence on a Native language as the lead one in *The Good Rainbow Road* is twofold: first, because the Indigenous, or First, languages of the Americas are Native American or Indian; and, second, because Keres is one of the First languages, I want its presence to be a manifestation of the fact that Native land, culture, and community are the original and primary evidence of the Western Hemisphere.

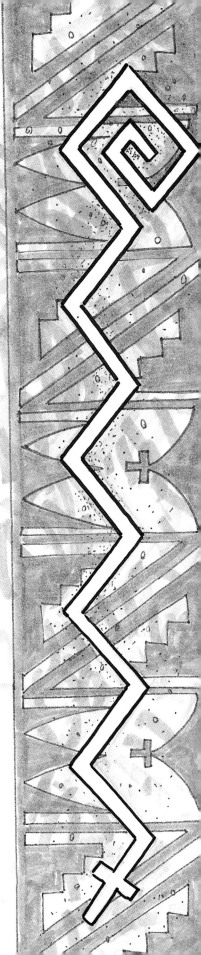

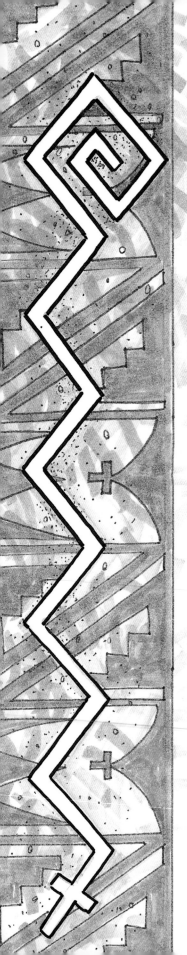

About the Author

Simon J. Ortiz is a poet, fiction writer, essayist, and storyteller. He is a native of Acoma Pueblo in New Mexico, where he grew up at Deetseyaamah, a rural village area in the Acoma Pueblo community. He is the father of three children—Raho, Rainy, and Sara—and is a grandfather. As a major Native writer, he insists on telling the story of his people's land, culture, and community, a story marred by social, political, economic, and cultural conflicts with Euro-American society. Ortiz's insistence, however, is upon a story that stresses vision and hope by creative struggle and resistance against human and technological oppression. His previous works include *Out There Somewhere, Men on the Moon, from Sand Creek, Speaking for the Generations, After and Before the Lightning, Woven Stone, The People Shall Continue,* and *Earth Power Coming.* He has received award recognition from the National Endowment for the Arts, Lila Wallace–Reader's Digest Fund Award, the Lannan Foundation's Artists in Residence, "Returning the Gift" Lifetime Achievement Award, WESTAF Lifetime Achievement Award, and the New Mexico Governor's Award for Excellence in Art. He lives in Toronto, Canada, where he is a Professor in the Department of English at the University of Toronto.

About the Illustrator

Michael Lacapa is of Apache, Hopi, and Tewa descent. He grew up on the Fort Apache Indian Reservation, where he first heard the old stories told by the elders. After completing high school, he attended Arizona State University, where he received a degree in secondary art education. He returned to the reservation to teach and to develop traditional stories into books. In 1981, Michael co-authored and illustrated his first book, *Ndee Benadogé'i: Three Stories of the White Mountain Apache Tribe.* Since then, Michael has illustrated and authored fourteen pieces of literature for the child in us all. Michael currently writes and illustrates with his wife Kathy and his son Anthony in Taylor, Arizona.

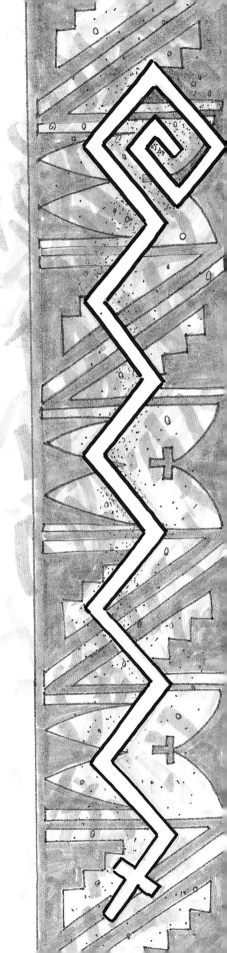

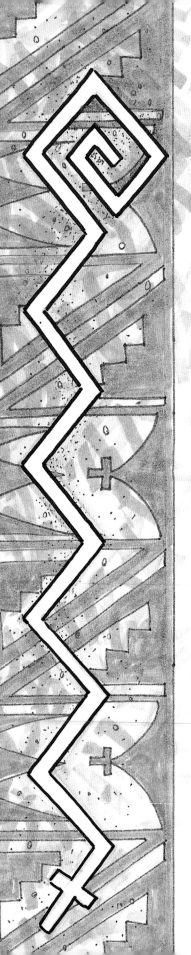

About Oyate

Oyate is a Native organization working to see that our lives and histories are portrayed honestly, and so that all people know our stories belong to us. Our work includes evaluation of texts, resource materials and fiction by and about Native peoples; conducting of teacher and community workshops, in which participants learn to evaluate children's books for honest portrayals of Native peoples; administration of a small resource center and library; distribution of children's, young adult and teacher materials, with an emphasis on writing and illustration by Native people; and an annual giveaway of the best in American Indian books to organizations serving Native children. Oyate may be contacted at www.oyate.org and by phone at (510) 848-6700.

We thank the LEF Foundation and the Threshold Foundation for their generous support in making the publication of this beautiful book possible.